?

Science, Maker, and Real Technology Students

S.M.A.R.T.S.

D1059345

#NERD

S.M.A.R.T.S. is published by Stone Arch Books
A Capstone Imprint
1710 Roe Crest Drive
North Mankato, MN 56003
www.mycapstone.com

Library of Congress Cataloging-in-Publication Data is available on the Library of Congress website.

ISBN: 978-1-4965-3016-5 (hardcover) — 978-1-4965-3018-9 (paperback) — 978-1-4965-3020-2 (ebook pdf)

Summary: After winning a contest, S.M.A.R.T.S. participates in a Mars colony simulation out in the desert. Now, only a day into the mission, the S.M.A.R.T.S. equipment is malfunctioning. Could it be sabotage?

Designer: Heidi Thompson

Printed in China.
007728

SRULE

S.M.A.R.T.S.

AND THE MARS MISSION MAYHEM

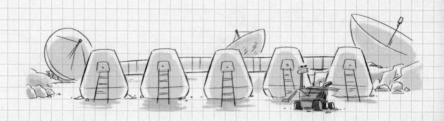

By Melinda Metz

Illustrated by Heath McKenzie

STONE ARCH BOOKS
a capstone imprint

1

"Who wants to go to Mars?" Mrs. Ramanujan asked once all the kids in S.M.A.R.T.S. — Science, Maker, and Real Technology Students — were on the field trip bus.

"Me! Me! Me! Did I say me?" Zoe Branson exclaimed. She wasn't sure if Mrs. Ram — that was what they usually called Hubble Middle School's fifth grade science teacher and the club's sponsor — could hear her. The other ten kids in S.M.A.R.T.S., including Zoe's best friends Caleb Quinn and Jaden Thompson, were shouting pretty much the same thing.

Joining S.M.A.R.T.S. was how Zoe, Caleb, and Jaden had become best friends. They'd been in classes together off and on since kindergarten. But this year, when they'd started the fifth grade, the three of them had joined the club. That's when they'd realized they all loved science and anything science-fiction related, including comics, video games, and movies.

Mrs. Ram grinned. "I really didn't need to ask, did I?"

Zoe grinned too. The S.M.A.R.T.S. had entered a contest for middle school science clubs and were one of four clubs that had won the chance to take part in a Mars mission simulation. Although they weren't actually going to Mars, this simulation was the next best thing.

The Mars Commission, the company who'd come up with the contest, wanted to put a colony on Mars one day and make the red planet a place where humans could live. Their headquarters were in Oregon's Alvord Desert, only a few hours from Hubble Middle School. The desert had some of the same environmental conditions as Mars. It was a great place to try out the habitats — the small buildings that Mars colonists would live in.

Four S.M.A.R.T.S. kids would actually be able to live in one of the habitats — habs for short — for four days. The rest of the club would be part of Mission Control, the group responsible for monitoring equipment and helping with any problems that came up. The other three clubs would each have their own habs and control centers.

As the bus pulled out of the parking lot, Mrs. Ram took an iPad out of her blue felt TARDIS purse. She was as big a nerd as the kids in the club, which made her all kinds of awesome.

"We'll use the Pick Me app to decide who our colonists will be," she told them. Mrs. Ram had preloaded the names of everyone in S.M.A.R.T.S. into the app and used it to select four kids at random. "Our Martians are . . . Goo, Samuel, Dylan, and Zoe!"

Goo — whose real name was Maya — turned around in her seat and slapped Zoe a high five. Everyone called her Goo because she could answer questions faster than Google. Dylan let out a whoop. Samuel looked like someone had switched on a light inside him.

"Big yay!" Zoe exclaimed. "But I wish you guys could be in the hab too," she told Caleb and Jaden, who were sharing the bus's long back seat with her.

"I'm good with it," Jaden answered. "The control centers have some of the same equipment NASA uses."

Caleb nodded. "Plus, we get a rover. It's like the most awesome remote-controlled car ever."

"Somebody needs to —" Benjamin started to yell out.

He looked at his twin, Samuel, but Samuel didn't say anything. The twins almost always completed each other's sentences. They were so alike that their nicknames were Thing One and Thing Two, after the Dr. Seuss characters.

Benjamin started again. "Somebody needs to —" He hesitated, waiting for Samuel to jump in. Then he finished the sentence himself. "— trade with Samuel."

"No, they don't," Samuel answered.

"But we need to —" Benjamin took a breath. "— be together."

"No, we don't," Samuel said, crossing his arms. "I want to be a Martian. I can be on my own."

"You're crazy! Mr. Leavey, tell Samuel he has to be on Mission Control with me," Benjamin said to the Hubble Middle School librarian.

Mr. Leavey turned around in his seat. He was almost like a second sponsor for S.M.A.R.T.S., which was why he was also on the field trip. He'd helped set up a makerspace with all kinds of tools and materials in the back of the media center for the kids to work on their projects.

"It's Samuel's decision," Mr. Leavey answered.

Zoe noticed that the librarian was wearing one green sock and one plaid sock. Typical Mr. Leavey. He always kept the library super neat, but he had trouble keeping himself the same way.

As the brothers argued quietly with each other, Jaden tried to remember if he'd ever seen one twin without the other. He was pretty sure he hadn't.

"There's no way the two of them can function apart," Caleb whispered to his friends.

Zoe nibbled on her bottom lip. She was afraid Caleb was right. What if Samuel couldn't handle the four days in the hab without Benjamin?

NERDS RULE

?

2

"I can't believe we have to share a bus with *them*,"
Sonja, the tallest — and feistiest — kid in S.M.A.R.T.S.
burst out as the bus came to a stop in front of Edison
Middle School.

The Edison science club, the Mad Scientists, was one
of the other teams taking part in the Mars simulation.
Since both clubs were from schools in the same town, their
sponsors had decided it made sense for them to share
a bus.

"They turned out to be pretty nice," Jaden argued. "They all congratulated us after we won that unsolved mystery competition between our clubs, remember?"

"Don't *you* remember that they cheated?" Sonja demanded. In the competition, both teams had been required to come up with a solution to an unsolved mystery. For S.M.A.R.T.S., part of solving the mystery had been figuring out that the Mad Scientists had tried to trick them.

"And not *all* of them were nice," Caleb added as the driver got out to help the Mads load their gear into the bus's storage compartment. "Not Barrett Snyder."

"Barrett's different," Zoe said. She looked out the window at him. Barrett was eating a giant bag of Cheez Crunchies and had orange crumbs all down the front of his shirt. "He's still mad that he didn't get to be in S.M.A.R.T.S."

Barrett was a former Hubble Middle School student who'd really wanted to join the S.M.A.R.T.S., but his grades hadn't been good enough. When he'd transferred to Edison earlier in the year, he'd joined the Mad Scientists right away. It seemed like his goal was proving the Mads were superior.

"Let's think of this as a fresh start," Mrs. Ram suggested, overhearing their conversation.

A few moments later, Mr. Olsen, the Mad Scientists' sponsor, led his club onto the bus. Barrett plopped down in a seat near the Things. He stuffed another handful of Crunchies into his mouth, then cracked his knuckles.

"Don't crack your knuckles. We —" Benjamin began.

This time Samuel jumped right in, "— hate that sound!"

Barrett grinned. "What, you mean *this* sound?" He cracked his knuckles again, and the Things let out a howl.

"Barrett, enough," Mr. Olsen said firmly.

"Yeah, Barrett," Amanda, one of the Mads, said. "That's so annoying."

Finn, another Mads, cleared his throat. "Uh, we all wanted to say again that we're sorry about the last competition."

Sonja frowned, but Jaden smiled. "Thanks," he said. Most of the other S.M.A.R.T.S. nodded.

During the ride, the Mads seemed like they were trying to be extra nice. One of the girls, Caroline, traded bad jokes with Jaden. Finn passed around a bag of homemade cookies while the two clubs talked about the Mars colony simulation. Amanda started up the license plate game, and almost everybody from both groups played.

Jaden noticed that Samuel and Benjamin didn't join in. They kept their heads close together, talking only to each other. Barrett didn't play, either.

"Look!" Mrs. Ram exclaimed after they'd been on the road a couple hours. "You can see the habs."

Zoe's heart started beating faster as the structures came into view. Each hab looked like a row of four giant marshmallows linked together by short elevated tunnels. She wished the bus could drive straight across the desert and right over to them. She wanted to explore!

"Do you think people could really live in those tiny habs for the rest of their lives?" Jaden asked.

"You sound scared," Barrett said with a sneer. "I bet you'd be crying to get out before the simulation ended, and it's only four days."

"Four days would be no problem," Jaden answered, his eyes on the habs. "But we're talking decades for the colonists."

"How about a bet?" Barrett asked the other Mad Scientists. "I say we'll handle the simulation a hundred times better than S.M.A.R.T.S. The sponsors can be the judges and pick which team does the best."

"It's not a competition, Barrett," Amanda reminded him. "It's a chance to experience what it would be like to live on another planet."

"You don't want to go up against us, anyway," Caleb added. "We crushed you in our last competition."

"Oooh, them's fightin' words," Caroline joked. "Now we *have* to do it." Finn and some of the other Mads nodded in agreement.

Amanda shrugged. "If everyone wants to . . . sure."

"We are so in!" Sonja called.

"If it's a competition, what's the prize?" Zoe asked. She was much more excited about living like a Mars colonist than competing, but a contest could be fun.

"We're all makers. I say losers make the winners a trophy," Caroline suggested.

"Then S.M.A.R.T.S. will have to make a trophy case for when we win," Jaden joked. He turned toward Mrs. Ram, Mr. Leavey, and Mr. Olsen. "Could you be our judges? Pretty please?"

The adults looked at each other. "You'll have to accept our decision with no arguments," Mr. Leavey said finally.

Both teams agreed. "But the Mad Scientists better not cheat again," Sonja added loudly.

3

"What's going on out there?" Caleb exclaimed as the bus finally came to a stop. In front of them was the massive Mars Commission building — and a huge group of people.

The crowd rushed over to the bus. They all wore T-shirts that said *Earth First* and most carried signs. Jaden could make out a few: *Mars: 35 million miles away. Homeless shelter: 24 miles away. Low tech = high happiness.*

"I read that there were groups against the Mars Commission colony," Mrs. Ram said. "But I wasn't expecting anything like this."

One of the protestors, a teenage girl with a long black braid, pounded on Zoe's window. She waved her sign wildly. It said: *Live Simply So That Others May Simply Live.*

"But why are they against the colony?" Zoe asked, trying to ignore the girl.

"Money," Mrs. Ram explained. "It would cost about six billion dollars just to get a team of four colonists on Mars. Some people think that money should be used to help those who are struggling right here on Earth."

"Don't they know that a lot of big scientists think the human race could die out if we don't find a way to live on other planets?" Caleb asked, raising his voice. He had to talk loudly. Someone was banging on his window now.

The protestors began to move back, and Jaden saw it was because a tall man with a buzz cut was leading a group of security guards over to the bus. A minute later, the bus door opened with a hiss.

The kids let Jaden walk to the front of the bus first. He needed a little extra time because he had cerebral palsy, CP, and used leg braces to help him walk. CP affected people in different ways. For Jaden, it made one of his arms and one of his legs stiff and hard to move.

"Earth First, Earth First!" the protestors chanted as the kids filed off the bus and into the dry desert air.

"Welcome, welcome!" the man with the buzz cut said, using a bullhorn to be heard over the chanting. "I'm your host, Timothy Pegg, CEO of the Mars Commission. This is Kaylee Phelps." Mr. Pegg gestured to the teenage girl next to him. "She's going to be writing about the simulation for her science blog."

Kaylee smiled, waving with one hand. She used the other to film the two clubs with her cell phone.

Mr. Pegg led the group past the protestors and toward the Mars Commission building. It looked like a bunch of gigantic glass building blocks of all different shapes that had been stacked into a tower. Tall glass doors slid open as they approached, and Mr. Pegg waved them inside.

"I apologize for those Earth First maniacs," Mr. Pegg said, gesturing toward the crowd outside. "Don't worry. They're a little nuts, but harmless. They —"

Mr. Pegg was interrupted by another outburst from The Things.

"He's doing —" Benjamin yelled.

"— it again!" Samuel cried. They both glared at Barrett.

Jaden noticed Kaylee was filming the twins with her cell. "He must have cracked his knuckles," he explained to the teen blogger as Mrs. Ram calmed down the Things and Mr. Olsen whispered something to Barrett. "The twins hate that sound, and he knows it."

"I get that," Kaylee replied. "I hate hearing a fork scrape against a plate." She smiled, and it was like a rainbow. Under her braces were colored tabs, a different color for each tooth.

The group followed Mr. Pegg, taking an elevator up to a conference room that took up the whole floor. The room was already filled with kids and adults.

"Here are our last two teams," Mr. Pegg announced. "Sit, sit," he urged the S.M.A.R.T.S. and the Mad Scientists, gesturing toward some empty white leather chairs.

Caleb, Zoe, and Jaden found seats together, and Kaylee plopped down next to them. Barrett sat down in the row behind them. He tapped Caleb on the shoulder.

"S.M.A.R.T.S. should just give up now," he said. "Samuel doesn't need the extra stress of a competition. You saw how he freaked out over a little knuckle cracking. Who knows how he'll deal without Thing One." He tilted back his head so he could empty the last of the Crunchies directly into his mouth.

"He'll be —" Zoe began.

"What competition?" Kaylee interrupted.

"Our teams have a friendly bet going about which team will do better in the simulation," Jaden explained as Kaylee turned her phone on him.

A man squeezed past, taking one of the last empty seats. "Who are all these people?" Zoe asked Kaylee.

"Besides the other two winning teams — the Kelvins and the Fig Neutrons — there are reporters and people who Mr. Pegg hopes will invest in the Mars Commission," Kaylee answered. "It costs big bucks to get a colony started and lots more to keep it going."

"Welcome again," Mr. Pegg said as he stepped up onto a raised platform at the front of the room. "I'm sure you're all eager to hear the details of the simulation, so I won't delay. We at the Mars Co—"

"There are people on Earth who need your money!" a voice shouted, cutting off Mr. Pegg.

Zoe looked back to see the girl with the black braid, the one who'd been pounding on her bus window, rushing off the elevator.

"If you don't care about that," the girl continued, "maybe you'll care that the Mars colony will fail. The plants he" — she pointed at Mr. Pegg — "is planning to grow will produce unsafe levels of oxygen in the habs. That could lead to spontaneous explosions."

There were murmurs from the group. Two security guards were already striding toward the girl, but she kept yelling: "And if the colonists aren't incinerated, they might starve. The calories from the crops aren't enough to —"

The guards each took one of the girl's elbows and hustled her back onto the elevator. "They aren't enough for people to li—" Her voice was cut off as the huge doors slid shut.

"Please excuse the interruption," Mr. Pegg said to the group. He forced a grin so huge Zoe thought she could see every tooth in his head. "The young lady clearly doesn't have accurate information. And how could she? The Earth Firsters hardly know the Internet exists."

A woman stood up. "I'm not sure I'm willing to invest in a project —" she began.

Mr. Pegg didn't let her finish. "Let's hold off on questions until you've had the chance to see our habitats in use by these bright kids. I'm sure you'll all be very impressed."

Caleb gave a soft snort. "Incineration. Starvation," he muttered. "I thought staying in the habitats was supposed to be a fantastic prize."

Zoe and Jaden exchanged a look. They both knew Caleb's favorite word was DOOM. He was always expecting some catastrophe to happen.

"Caleb, don't be so . . . so *Caleb*," Zoe said, giving his arm a reassuring pat. "Nothing bad is going to happen."

4

"It's like being in a high-tech hobbit hole," Zoe said as Mr. Pegg led her, Goo, Dylan, and Samuel through the hab several hours later. He was giving them a tour of what would be their home for the next four days.

Mr. Pegg had already shown them what was inside three of the modules — the rounded, puffy sections of the hab that had made Zoe think of marshmallows when she saw them from the bus. The bedrooms and bathroom were in one, the lab/exercise room was in another, and the common room, where they could all hang out and relax, was in the third.

Zoe wanted to spend every free second she had in the lab. She couldn't wait to try out all the neat scientific equipment. She, Goo, Samuel, and Dylan had all been given a science experiment to work on — Zoe's experiment was studying worms.

They'd also need to put in an hour a day on the treadmill that was at one end of the lab module. Real colonists would have to exercise to keep their bones and muscles strong in Mars's lower gravity. And for the next three days, they were colonists!

"The last module is your galley, or kitchen," Mr. Pegg said, leading them inside. "There's a fridge, freezer, microwave, oven, and stove. The oven and stove won't be functioning during the simulation, but you will get to use the food rehydrator." He touched what looked like a drawer underneath a cabinet.

"Awesome possum! We get to eat dehydrated astronaut food!" Zoe exclaimed.

"But aren't the colonists going to be growing their own food?" Dylan asked.

"Ultimately, yes, but the greenhouse modules aren't ready yet," Mr. Pegg said. "And the colonists won't have any crops when they first arrive on Mars, so they'll need to bring dehydrated food. It's light, so they can bring more of it. As colonists, you'll need to be aware of how quickly you use up your supplies. There's advice on food rationing in your mission binders."

Just then, Kaylee squeezed into the crowded room. "Sorry. I let you get ahead of me again. There's just so much stuff in here that I want to show on my blog." She rubbed the screen of her cell with the hem of her shirt and started taking more pictures. Zoe noticed the screen left an orange streak on the blogger's clothing.

"Well, this is the end of the tour. Any questions before you begin your Mars mission?" Mr. Pegg asked.

"Oh, I do! What happens if the hab equipment breaks?" Kaylee asked.

Mr. Pegg frowned, then quickly flashed a big smile. "I have complete confidence in our equipment," he answered. "But if something does go wrong with one of the systems during the simulation — which is very unlikely — we've made sure the habs will still be supplied with oxygen, heat, and everything else the kids need. They'll be perfectly safe."

"And we'll have Mission Control," Zoe reminded Kaylee. "They'll help us figure out any problems. We're even wearing monitors so they can watch our vital signs." She ran her fingers over one of the electrodes taped to her skin.

"Are there any other questions from our *colonists*?" Mr. Pegg asked, turning toward the S.M.A.R.T.S.

Zoe was sure she'd think of a million questions later, but they'd have their binder — and Goo, who remembered everything she read. "I think we're good," she answered. The other three nodded.

"Great!" Mr. Pegg clapped his hands. "See you when you return to Earth."

"Good luck!" Kaylee said. She turned and followed Mr. Pegg through the tight tunnel that led out of the hab.

The S.M.A.R.T.S. colonists were all alone.

Goo had already sat at the table and started flipping through the binder. "Okay, so our most important job is keeping the hab operating smoothly. It's the only thing protecting us."

"Protecting us from . . . what?" Samuel asked.

"You know. The stuff we've been talking about since we won the contest," Goo answered. "The average temperature on Mars is negative eighty degrees Fahrenheit. The atmosphere is only about one percent of Earth's atmosphere. That means a lot less protection from radiation. And Mars's atmosphere is only about 0.2 percent oxygen," she rattled off.

"On Earth, the atmosphere is twenty-six percent oxygen," Dylan added. "So basically if we went outside without protective gear, we'd freeze to death, suffocate, and get radiation poisoning."

Zoe shivered. She was excited to be in the hab. After all, being an astronaut was her dream. But it was a little scary imagining living on a planet that was so dangerous.

NERDS RULE

?

5

"I feel like I'm working at NASA," Jaden said from his console in the control center. He, Caleb, Sonja, and Benjamin were alone in the S.M.A.R.T.S. Mission Control, ready to start the simulation. The control centers for the other groups were all on the second floor of the Mars Commission building — Mads and S.M.A.R.T.S. on the west wing, and the Kelvins and Fig Neutrons on the east.

"Me too," Caleb agreed, sitting down at the console next to Jaden. A row of monitors was set up in front of him.

The four S.M.A.R.T.S. kids were taking the first Mission Control shift, which meant they would be watching over the colonists in the hab for the next eight hours. Antonio, Destiny, and Brooke were taking the night shift, which started at two thirty in the morning.

While the colonists had been getting a tour of the hab, one of the Mars Commission engineers had been going over the control center's equipment with the rest of the S.M.A.R.T.S., plus Mrs. Ram and Mr. Leavey. She had also explained that all communication between Mission Control and the colonists would be on a twelve-minute delay.

Although emails could be sent almost instantly on Earth, communication between Mars and Earth wouldn't be so easy. Messages couldn't travel faster than the speed of light, and Mars was between 34.8 million to 250 million miles from Earth, depending on where the two planets were in their rotations around the Sun.

That meant a message could take anywhere from 3 to 22.5 minutes to go from one planet to the other. In order to make the simulation realistic, Mr. Pegg had decided it should take twelve minutes to receive emails or other communications.

After they'd gone over the Mission Control basics, Antonio, Destiny, and Brooke had gone upstairs to rest in the huge suite that S.M.A.R.T.S. had been assigned. Then Mrs. Ram and Mr. Leavey had left too. The sponsors were allowed in the control center, but Mr. Pegg wanted the kids to handle the simulation on their own. The Mission Control team had Mrs. Ram and Mr. Leavey's cell numbers if they needed anything.

"Okay, so what do we do first?" Sonja asked.

"How about if we each monitor one colonist?" Jaden suggested. They wouldn't be using all the tech in the room, but they'd be able to monitor the most important functions of the hab and keep watch on the colonists' vital signs. "We can divide up the hab systems too, so we won't have to try to watch everything at once."

"I'll take . . . Samuel," Benjamin said. He was still pausing in the middle of every sentence, as if Samuel would be jumping in to finish it.

They quickly divided up the rest of the hab team. Sonja would monitor Goo. Jaden would monitor Dylan. Caleb would monitor Zoe.

"Samuel's stressed!" Benjamin exclaimed as he brought up his twin's vitals. "Blood pressure . . . is one hundred and thirty over ninety. Heart rate . . . ninety-four beats per minute. I knew he should . . . have traded."

"Those levels aren't dangerous," Sonja pointed out.

"But Benjamin's levels might be," Caleb muttered to Jaden.

Jaden glanced over. Benjamin's forehead was sweaty, and he seemed to be blinking faster than usual. He definitely looked stressed!

"Hey, look!" Sonja exclaimed. "They're coming into the common room! It seems like everyone's okay."

The common room was the only part of the hab with a camera that sent a video feed back to the control center. They all watched the screen as Zoe, Goo, Dylan, and Samuel sat down in padded chairs.

"What is Samuel doing?" Caleb yelled, jumping to his feet. "He's eating Cheez Crunchies!"

"So? We really . . . like them," Benjamin said.

"But *crumbs*!" Caleb replied, running over to the screen. He tapped it to enlarge the image of Samuel. Big orange crumbs had fallen onto the twin's shirt.

Jaden felt like an alarm bell had started ringing in his head. "Crumbs could get into the CO_2 scrubber," he explained. "They might really mess up the machine. And if the scrubber is broken, the air will become unsafe to breathe!"

The colonists produced carbon dioxide, or CO_2, every time they exhaled. The invisible gas had to be taken out of the air and vented outside the hab by a special gadget called the CO_2 scrubber. If too much carbon dioxide filled the sealed hab, there wouldn't be enough oxygen left for the colonists to breathe.

"Why does he even have Crunchies?" Caleb moaned. "Astronauts don't get to bring food like that. They can't even have bread. They use tortillas for sandwiches. Crumbs can be deadly!"

"I don't . . . get it. I packed . . . both our bags. No Crunchies," Benjamin answered. Then he started blinking even faster. "Someone else must've put Crunchies in Samuel's bag!" He spoke loudly and without any more hesitation. "It was Barrett!"

"Let's go find that stinking cheater!" Sonja cried, already starting for the door.

"No!" Jaden rolled his desk chair into the aisle to block her. "We don't know he did it."

"Who else could it be?" Benjamin demanded.

Jaden thought for a second. "The Earth Firsters!" he exclaimed. "I bet they'd love for the Mars Commission to look bad in front of all the reporters and possible investors. Maybe they're trying to mess up the simulation."

"That would make sense," Caleb agreed. "But Barrett is still a good suspect. We know he doesn't have a problem with playing dirty."

"We'll figure it out," Jaden promised. "Just not now. We're Mission Control. Our first job is to help the colonists."

Sonja huffed out a frustrated breath, then nodded. "You're right. They need to know not to eat any more Crunchies."

"I'll email Samuel!" Benjamin volunteered.

"We're probably too late," Caleb said.

"What are you talking about?" Benjamin asked. His fingers were already flying over the keyboard.

"Remember the delay? It'll take twelve minutes for the message to get to them. And the video we're getting is on a twelve-minute delay too," Caleb explained. "Which means Benjamin was actually eating the Crunchies twelve minutes before we saw him do it. He's probably already finished the whole bag."

"I forgot about that," Benjamin said. He hit the send button so hard it made a popping sound. "I forgot how far away Mars really is."

6

The first thing Zoe thought about when she woke up in her tiny bedroom Saturday morning was the CO_2 scrubber. She'd been worrying about it ever since they got that email from Mission Control last night. She couldn't believe she and the other colonists hadn't thought about the damage the Crunchies crumbs might do.

Zoe climbed out of her bunk, got dressed, and walked through the short tunnel to the common room. She checked the stats on the hab's atmosphere. The carbon dioxide levels were fine — for now.

She sat down in front of a monitor to check her email. Nothing official from Mission Control, but there were messages from other S.M.A.R.T.S., cheering the colonists on. There was also an email from Mr. Pegg:

To: zoebranson@marscommission.com

From: timpegg@marscommisssion.com

Hi, Zoe!

I hope you're enjoying the experience of being a Mars colonist. Traveling to Mars, you would have already spent more than six months with your three crewmates.

One of the difficulties of being a colonist is living in such close quarters — even with your friends. To make our simulation as realistic as it can be, I have a request. It may sound strange, but I'd like you to crack your knuckles at least twice an hour. Many people find the sound irritating. These kind of minor annoyances can become a huge problem on Mars.

I hope you'll help me out with this, Zoe. I'm so pleased to have you as one of the first people to live in our habs.

Sincerely,

Tim Pegg

Zoe stared at the email for a few moments, then closed it. She'd read tons about life as an astronaut, and she knew Mr. Pegg was right about how hard it was to live in a small space with other people.

Still . . . Zoe nibbled her lip. She didn't want to do anything that would bug Goo, Dylan, and Samuel, but it *would* make the simulation more realistic. Maybe it could help the Mars Commission better prepare the real colonists. She decided she'd do it.

"Hi," came a voice.

Zoe looked over her shoulder and saw Goo. "Hi," she answered.

Keeping her eyes locked on Goo, Zoe cracked her knuckles. The sound didn't seem to bother Goo. She had the right kind of personality for a colonist — she didn't get upset much.

"First thing on our schedule is breakfast," Zoe said. "Want to go rehydrate something?"

"Sure," Goo said. "I just want to check my email first."

Zoe nodded while she logged out. "See you in there."

When Zoe reached the small galley, she found Dylan and Samuel going through the foil packages of food.

"I'm going for the Mexican scrambled eggs," Dylan announced. He moved out of the way so Zoe could look at the choices, then slid the top of his package into the rehydrator. He selected the number of milliliters of water needed, chose hot, and then started the machine. "My mom should get one of these," he said when he pulled the package free and tore it open.

"You aren't supposed to open it right away," Goo told him as she joined them in the galley. "The package tells you how long to wait. Didn't you read the directions?" Zoe noticed that Goo's voice was sharper than usual.

Dylan frowned as he looked into the package. "Gross. I'm throwing it away and starting over."

"You can't. The food is rationed. We only get to eat a certain amount a day," Zoe reminded him. "There's no mini-mart to walk to on Mars."

"I'll go hungry then," Dylan snapped. "It smells terrible anyway."

"I thought dinner was good last night," she replied, cracking her knuckles. Samuel flinched.

Uh-oh, Zoe thought. She'd forgotten how much Samuel hated that sound. And she had to crack her knuckles twice an hour!

"You can have my food," Samuel told Dylan. "I'm not hungry." He glared at Zoe, then stomped out of the galley.

He's a lot more than just irritated, Zoe thought, staring after Samuel and feeling worried. To win the competition, she, Samuel, Dylan, and Goo needed to work as a team. But could they do that when it was obvious that Samuel couldn't even stand to be in the same room with her?

7

After breakfast, Caleb and Jaden decided to investigate the Cheez Crunchies mystery before their next Mission Control shift. Step one was to check out the Earth Firsters.

When they walked out of the huge front doors, they spotted the protestors sitting in groups by a row of tents. "So do we just walk up to them?" Caleb asked. "Or do we —"

"I think the decision's been made for us," Jaden answered. The girl with the long black braid was trotting toward them, a bag slung over one shoulder. A younger girl with the same long black hair was with her.

"Hi, I'm Robin. You're some of the contest winners, right?" the girl said, coming to a stop in front of them.

Caleb nodded slowly. "Yeah, I'm Caleb, and this is Jaden."

"Nice to meet you," she replied, smiling. "We're having breakfast. You want to eat with us?"

Jaden raised his eyebrows. "Seriously?"

"Seriously. It'll be good too. Everything's locally grown. Did you know that they've started growing quinoa around here?" Robin asked.

"I don't even know what quinoa is," Jaden admitted.

"It's a kind of grain," Robin explained.

The younger girl made a face and pretended to gag. "Hey, do you guys have smart phones?" she asked. "You must. Everybody has one, if their parents aren't crazy."

"Lark, no!" Robin exclaimed.

"What?" Lark said. "If I borrow a phone, I didn't buy it, so I didn't use money that could be used to help people. I borrow my friends' at school. Please just let me borrow one." She looked back and forth between Caleb and Jaden. "I want to get to the next level of Bubble Witch."

"They aren't giving you a phone," Robin said firmly. She turned back toward the boys. "So, breakfast?"

Caleb eyed Robin suspiciously. "It seemed like you didn't want us around when we showed up yesterday," he said. "And now you're inviting us to breakfast?"

"We don't have anything against you," Robin answered. "We just don't want some company spending billions of dollars on something stupid when there are so many people who need so much right here."

"But every space mission has led to amazing new technology," Jaden protested. "Like the research NASA has done on artificial muscle systems for their space robots has given people better prosthetic limbs. Firefighting gear used all over the country is based on lightweight materials that were developed for our space program. And —"

"And did you know that forty-nine million people in the U.S. have trouble getting enough food?" Robin interrupted. "Let me give you one of our pamphlets." She dug around in her bag, spilling stuff onto the ground — a hairbrush, a library book, and a packet of Cheez Crunchies!

Caleb picked it up. "Wow. I didn't know they had Crunchies trees in the U.S.!" he exclaimed.

Lark giggled. Robin snatched the Crunchies away from Caleb. "Those aren't mine!" she snapped.

"Then why were they in your bag?" Jaden's voice was calm, but his Spidey senses were tingling. Could Robin be the one who'd put the Crunchies in Samuel's bag?

A blush spread up Robin's neck and into her face. "It belonged to someone in my group," she admitted. "I confiscated it."

"She's like the Earth First police," Lark whispered.

"Look," Robin insisted, "not everyone in Earth First is perfect. But we're still right about how it's horrible to waste a bunch of money going to Mars!"

Robin shoved the Cheez Crunchies into her bag, then grabbed the rest of her stuff off the ground. She took Lark's hand and hurried away.

"I guess we're not getting our second breakfast," Caleb commented.

"That's okay," Jaden said. "She gave us something even better — a clue!"

8

"Guys, I think crumbs did get in the scrubber!" Sonja exclaimed from her station in the S.M.A.R.T.S. control center. It was about an hour after she, Caleb, Jaden, and Benjamin had started their second shift as Mission Control.

"Why? What's happening?" Benjamin cried.

"I just took a reading on the atmosphere in the hab," Sonja explained. "The CO_2 is up. And if the amount of CO_2 continues to rise at the same rate, the hab will run out of oxygen in a little more than two days and three hours."

"They won't have enough air to last until Monday afternoon!" Benjamin said. "We have to get them out right now." He pulled out his cell and started to bring up Mrs. Ram's number.

"What's happening in the hab is just a simulation," Jaden pointed out. "The hab will always have enough air and heat. The reading is telling us what would be happening if the scrubber damage really affected the amount of oxygen. Samuel and the others are fine."

"But if we want to win the contest, we have to act like the simulation is real. No oxygen in the hab equals automatic failure," Caleb said.

"You're right," Jaden agreed. "We need to figure this out — soon." He clicked a few keys, and a clock appeared on one of the screens. It started ticking down from fifty-one hours.

50:59:60.

50:59:59.

50:59:58.

Jaden couldn't take his eyes off the numbers as the seconds slipped away. With each second that went by, the colonists were closer to running out of air.

* * *

About an hour later, Caleb and Sonja were crowded around Jaden's monitor, studying a diagram of the scrubber. They'd emailed the colonists telling them that Mission Control would come up with a fix for the machine. The first step was learning exactly how it worked.

"Okay, so the fan blows air from the hab over a bed full of pellets," Caleb said. "Then the CO_2 sticks to the pellets." He shook his head. "I don't get why the CO_2 sticks."

The three of them stared at the screen in silence. Benjamin wasn't even listening. He just stared at Samuel's vital signs on his monitor.

Sonja typed out a search. "The pellets are made from this mineral called zeolite," she said. "Check out this drawing of its molecular structure."

Jaden gave a low whistle. "Close up, zeolite looks like it's filled with cages."

"I get it," Caleb said. "Those cages trap small molecules. Carbon dioxide sticks to the pellets in the scrubber because the molecules get caught in the holes in the zeolite."

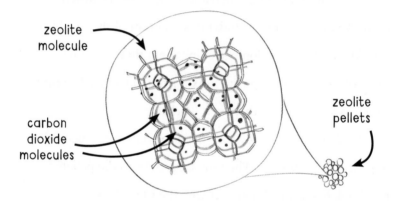

zeolite molecule

carbon dioxide molecules

zeolite pellets

Sonja let out a long breath. "The scrubber has a cool design. Except the part where it isn't working."

"It's got to be the fan that's messed up, right?" Jaden said. "If crumbs get in a scrubber, they can get caught up in the fan's motor or the axle."

"Right, and that would slow the fan down," Caleb answered. "If the fan isn't spinning as fast as it should be, it won't blow as much air over the pellets, and the pellets won't soak up as much CO_2. The scrubber is still working — just not that well."

"So can we just have them open the scrubber up and clean the fan?" Sonja asked.

"Too risky," Caleb said, running his fingers through his hair. "They'd have to shut down the scrubber to open it up. Who knows how long it would take them to clean the fan and get it going again. They could run out of oxygen before they finish."

"We can figure out how to make a new fan out of stuff they have in the hab and send them instructions," Jaden said. "Then they'll only have to shut the scrubber down long enough to open it up and put in the new fan."

"Are you sure we can make a fan?" Sonja asked doubtfully.

"We can do it," Jaden said, trying to sound confident. "This isn't any different than if we were back in our makerspace working on a project."

"I still say we should just have them come out now," Benjamin muttered from his station. "It's hopeless."

* * *

Jaden glanced at what Caleb had started calling the Clock of DOOM. Time was ticking: 46:13:32.

The Mission Control team had come up with a list of things from the hab that would make good building materials for the fan. Mrs. Ram and Mr. Leavey had gotten everything on the list from Mars Commission engineers and had dropped off the supplies.

For more than three hours, Jaden, Caleb, and Sonja had been trying to figure out how to make the replacement fan. But so far, they hadn't come up with anything.

Jaden rubbed his scalp. Maybe he needed better blood flow to his brain. The ideas just weren't coming. He smiled when the door opened and Mrs. Ram came in. She couldn't help, but seeing her somehow made him feel like they could work out the problem.

"Cookies and drinks," Mrs. Ram announced, holding up a large bag. "How's it going?"

Caleb groaned. Sonja growled. "We're stuck right now," Jaden admitted. "But when we get stuck on a project in the makerspace, we eventually figure it out."

"But with those projects, there isn't a time limit. There isn't —" Benjamin jerked his head back toward his monitor. "An email just came in from Samuel!"

"Read it!" Sonja urged.

Benjamin began to read aloud:

To: benjaminwestbury@marscommission.com

From: samuelwestbury@marscommission.com

Maybe you were right. Maybe I should've traded so I didn't have to be in the hab. Everyone is driving me crazy. Zoe won't stop cracking her knuckles. Dylan is complaining about the food and everything else. Goo is criticizing everybody.

Plus I got an email from Mr. Pegg this morning. He told me that in order to make the sim more real, I should spend more time in the shower than we're supposed to. We're only allowed two minutes each to save water. But he said in a real mission, we'd all be doing annoying things, and we'd have to learn to deal.

So after breakfast I did it. Everybody is mad at me. Everybody is mad at everybody. It doesn't even feel like we're a team anymore. The Mads might actually win.

"I don't care if the Mads win," Benjamin burst out when he'd finished reading. "We need to get Samuel out of there." He started tapping his heel against the floor.

"He didn't say he wanted out," Jaden said. "He sounded kind of frustrated but okay."

"Even on a regular day, Samuel needs me around," Benjamin declared. "You don't know." He glanced wildly around the room. "None of you know. It's a twin thing."

"It's okay, Benjamin. I'm going to take care of this," Mrs. Ram said firmly. "I'm calling Mr. Pegg right now. I don't approve of him using kids in what's basically a psychological experiment. I'll be right back."

"The Ram is on it, Benjamin," Sonja said. "You don't have to worry."

Benjamin's heel tapping slowed down . . . a little.

"Do you think Zoe could have gotten an email from Mr. Pegg too?" Jaden asked. "Benjamin said she kept cracking her knuckles. I don't think I've ever seen Zoe do that. And she knows it bothers him."

Caleb sat up straight. "Maybe all the colonists got emails. Samuel said Goo keeps criticizing everyone. Goo's not mean like that."

"And I don't see Dylan complaining about food," Sonja added. "In third grade, we used to call him Dylan the Disposal, remember? If you ever had anything in your lunch you didn't like, Dylan would eat it."

A few minutes later, Mrs. Ram strode back into the room. "This is so strange," she said. "Mr. Pegg said he didn't send emails to any of the kids on any of the teams."

Caleb felt his guts twisting into knots. "If Mr. Pegg didn't do it, then who did?"

9

"Samuel and the others will know the messages from Mr. Pegg are fakes in about three minutes," Jaden said.

As soon as Mrs. Ram had told them about the emails, Mission Control had sent out messages to all their colonists. Then Mrs. Ram had left to tell Mr. Olsen and the other team sponsors what had happened.

"Barrett is out to get our colonists," muttered Benjamin.

"I don't know, the Earth Firsters are looking pretty suspicious. We found a possible clue at their camp this morning," Caleb said. He and Jaden told the others about the Crunchies in Robin's bag.

"Could it be someone from one of the other teams?" Sonja asked. "It would be easy for them to get the other colonists' email addresses. They're all just the person's name plus marscommission.com."

Benjamin shook his head. "The competition is only between us and the Mads. The other teams don't have any reason to mess with our colonists."

Caleb rolled his chair over next to Jaden's. "Do you think Benjamin could be the perp?" he whispered. "He wanted Samuel to trade so they could be on Mission Control together, and it's freaking him out that they're separated. Now he keeps saying we should pull him out of the hab because of the sabotage."

Jaden's brows drew together as he thought. "It would've been easy for him to put the Crunchies in Samuel's bag," he whispered back.

"And he could've easily sent the emails from his console," Caleb said.

Jaden nodded. "I'll start a suspect list. So far we have Barrett and that protester, Robin." He hesitated a few seconds, then added, "And Benjamin."

* * *

Hours later, the S.M.A.R.T.S. were still stumped. It was almost the end of their Mission Control shift, and they still hadn't figured out who was behind the sabotage or how to make a new fan for the scrubber.

"Let's go through the materials again," Jaden said. He couldn't think of anything else to do. Maybe because it was so late — after two a.m.

Sonja yawned, then started pointing at the items they'd laid out on the back table. "We have the treadmill belt. We have —"

BANG! The door flew open, loudly hitting the wall. Barrett stormed in. Kaylee was right behind him, filming with her cell.

"You're the cheaters this time!" Barrett yelled. "I know about the emails you sent the Mads colonists, pretending to be Mr. Pegg. Very smart creating a bogus Mars Commission email account to send them from. You probably thought no one would notice that extra *s* in *commission*, but we did."

Caleb stared at Barrett in surprise. He couldn't believe that he and the others hadn't noticed the fake account. They hadn't even thought to check where the emails had been sent from!

"You tried to turn the Mads colonists against each other so we'd lose," Barrett continued.

"We did not! That's what you did to us!" Benjamin shot back.

"What are you talking about?" Barrett shouted. Kaylee continued to film, a little smile tugging at her lips.

Benjamin hit a few keys and brought up the email from his brother. "Look. It says right there that Samuel got an email from Mr. Pegg telling him to use too much water."

Barrett frowned as he read the email on Benjamin's monitor. "You guys probably sent fake emails to your own team too," he said. "That way no one would suspect you. But your colonists must've known to ignore the emails."

"I checked with the Fig Neutrons and the Kelvins after Mrs. Ram told everyone about the fake emails," Kaylee said. "They never got any — only the Mads and S.M.A.R.T.S. colonists did. It seems like somebody's cheating in the competition between your two teams."

"And it's him," Benjamin cried, pointing at Barrett. "Once a cheater, always a cheater."

As the two boys continued to argue, Caleb turned to Jaden. "Okay, Sherlock, what are you thinking?" he asked. Jaden was a complete Sherlock Holmes fanboy.

"Barrett could have done what he was accusing us of. He could've sent the emails to our team *and* his own team so he wouldn't look guilty," Jaden said, then shook his head. "But that would mean all the Mads were in on it. If they weren't, the emails would mess up their team too. I don't know if Barrett could have gotten all of them to agree to cheat. Most of them were really friendly on the bus."

Caleb frowned. "And what about Benjamin? Sending emails to the Mads wouldn't get Samuel out of the hab early. Why would he do that?"

"To make the competition fair, maybe?" Jaden suggested. "Both teams would have to deal with the same problem. He —"

Ping! Ping! One of the monitors sounded a warning, interrupting Jaden.

Benjamin gave a yelp and hit a couple keys on his computer. "The CO_2 in the hab is at 0.7 percent. It's rising even faster than we thought!"

"Huh? What's going on?" Barrett asked.

"What's going on is that the Crunchies you snuck into my brother's bag broke our scrubber," Benjamin replied. "Are you happy?"

"I didn't —" Barrett began.

"Just get out of here," Sonja told him.

Barrett scowled, then turned around and left without another word.

"He's probably heading off to sabotage us more," Benjamin muttered.

"But the Earth Firsters are still good suspects too, remember?" Jaden said.

"The Earth Firsters? Why?" Kaylee asked.

"Robin, one of the protestors, had some Cheez Crunchies," he told her. "She could've put a packet in Samuel's bag. If the Earth Firsters can mess up the simulation, it might make people think the Mars colony will fail. Mars Commission would be ruined if they can't get investors."

"Interesting," Kaylee said. "I hadn't thought of that."

"Earth Firsters, Barrett — doesn't really matter. Whoever the perp is, I don't think they're done," Benjamin said as he turned back to his monitor. "Something else is going to happen. Maybe something even worse than the wrecked scrubber."

"So what does the CO_2 level increasing mean for your team?" Kaylee asked, turning slowly, filming each of them.

"If it keeps going up at this rate, our team only has about nineteen hours of breathable air left," Benjamin told her. He reset the Clock of DOOM.

18:57:00.

10

Jaden, Caleb, Sonja, and Benjamin walked back into the control center Sunday morning at ten thirty. The first thing Jaden did was check the countdown clock: 10:29:03.

"How are the CO_2 levels doing?" Sonja asked the late-night Mission Control group.

Antonio stood up from his console and stretched. "They stayed steady," he replied. "And as far as we know, there wasn't any more sabotage."

"But we weren't able to figure out how to make a fan from this stuff," Destiny admitted. She and Brooke stood by the table in the back that they'd been using as their makerspace.

"Our turn," Sonja told them. "You guys have to get some sleep."

As the other S.M.A.R.T.S. headed for the door, Benjamin plopped down in front of his monitor. He obviously wasn't going to help — again.

Is it because he wants us to fail? Jaden wondered. *Does he want Samuel out of the hab that badly?*

"How about this?" Caleb asked from where he and Sonja stood at the makerspace table. He held up one of the food packets. "The outside might make good fan blades."

Sonja nodded. "That would work, but the blades aren't the hard part. The hard part is building the motor that spins the blades." She looked down at the table. So did Jaden and Caleb.

"Maybe we could —" Caleb began. He shook his head. "Never mind."

Suddenly Sonja straightened up. Her eyes glittered with excitement. "I think — yeah, I think this could work!" She picked up a miniature flashlight made up of six LED lights attached to a 9-volt battery. She pulled off the block of lights and held up the battery. "We can use this — and this." She grabbed some copper wire.

"By Odin's beard, she's going to make an electromagnet!" Caleb exclaimed, using one of Thor's favorite expressions.

Electromagnets were different than permanent magnets, like the ones used to hold stuff on a fridge. Electromagnets were created by running electric current through a wire. Lots of things were powered by electromagnets — doorbells, speakers, hard drives, and *fans*!

Benjamin got up from his console and walked over to the table. "That could actually work," he said. He took the wire from Sonja and started wrapping it around his finger to make a circle of coiled wire.

He's actually helping! Jaden thought. Good. He didn't want Benjamin to be the perp.

"Great!" Caleb told Benjamin. "Every loop of wire will make the electromagnet stronger. And the stronger the magnet is, the faster we can make our fan spin." It felt like they were back in the media center, teaming up to make something.

"We need a permanent magnet too," Jaden said. He scanned the table and quickly found one.

They would tape the permanent magnet to the battery from the flashlight. Two magnets always attracted or repelled each other. The push and pull between the electromagnet and the permanent magnet would make the wire spin. Then all they'd have to do was make some blades to attach to one end of the wire, and they'd have a working fan!

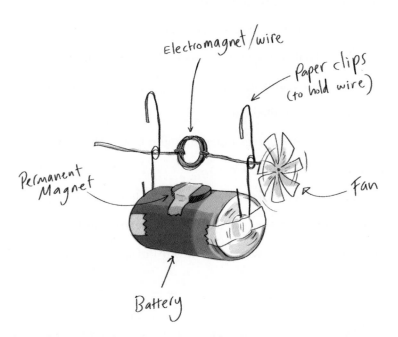

Electromagnet/wire

Paper clips
(to hold wire)

Permanent
Magnet

Fan

Battery

Back in the hab, Zoe held the fan they'd cut out of a dehydrated food package while Dylan attached it to one end of the copper wire. They were following the instructions that had arrived from Mission Control just over an hour ago.

"I hope this works," Goo said. "We only have about six hours and forty-five minutes of oxygen left!"

"We're all done," Zoe said when Dylan had finished.

"Let's try it!" Samuel exclaimed.

He bent a paper clip to hold each end of the wire. Then he taped one clip to the positive end of the battery and one to the negative end, sending a current through the wire and creating an electromagnet.

The fan began to spin! The four colonists cheered.

"Now all we have to do is just put it inside the scrubber," Zoe said.

It was easy to remove the cover from the wall of the hab, and there was room inside the scrubber for the new fan without removing the old one. They decided to leave it. It was still spinning, just slower than it should, so it would also help move air over the pellets.

"Now what?" Dylan asked after they'd screwed the cover back on.

"Now we send a message to Mission Control saying the fan is in place," Samuel said. "Then I say we follow our regular schedule while we wait to see if the CO_2 levels go down. That'll tell us if the scrubber's working."

"We make a great team," Zoe said. "I don't know who keeps sabotaging us, but we're solving every problem they throw at us. And I'm *really* glad we're not trying to annoy each other anymore."

Goo smiled. "And if our team fixed the scrubber, we'll win the contest for sure!"

* * *

"How are my little worms?" Zoe crooned half an hour later as she looked at her monitor in the lab. It showed video feeds from the three worm cultivation chambers attached to the counter on her left.

She, Dylan, Samuel, and Goo had each been assigned an experiment to work on while they were staying in the hab. If Zoe was really on Mars, the data collected from her worms could help show how the high levels of radiation on Mars might affect colonists.

"You should see them go," she told Samuel, who was busy putting in his time on the treadmill at the other end of the lab.

Zoe smiled as she watched the worms wiggle across the screen of her monitor. Then the image flickered and went black. The lights in the room dimmed for a moment, and Samuel's treadmill slowed down. He hit the stop button and climbed off.

"That was weird," he said. "The speed just suddenly dropped."

Goo appeared in the doorway, Dylan right behind her. "I just tried to send an email to Sonja to say hi, and it wouldn't go through. It's like there's no signal," she said.

"My computer —" Zoe began. Then all the lights went out. "Houston, we have a problem."

11

"What do we do?" Dylan asked.

Zoe peered through the darkness, trying to see his face. "I don't know," she admitted. She gripped the counter with both hands, almost afraid to move. It seemed like every machine in the hab was pinging or bleeping or ringing.

Thankfully, the backup generator kicked in a few minutes later, and some of the light returned to the lab. Zoe let her breath out in a whoosh.

"Goo, what did the binders say about power?" Samuel asked.

"There are emergency situations where the power will cut off. It can take up to two hours to get it back online," Goo answered. "But there *is* a backup. That's why we have lights again. The hab has batteries that are charged by nuclear reactors. Or at least that's how they'll be charged on Mars. The batteries don't have enough power to keep everything running, though."

"So we only use power for life support," Samuel said.

"We need heat too," Zoe said. "Remember, it's minus eighty outside."

Samuel thought for a moment. "The hab has four modules," he began. "We don't need heat in all of them. We can all stay in one until we get the power situation figured out."

Zoe was impressed. Samuel was really stepping up — even without his twin brother. "Let's get to work on the circuits," she said. "We'll cut power to everything we don't absolutely need."

"I can't believe this. Someone is definitely out to get us," Dylan said. "First someone snuck Crunchies into Samuel's bag. Then we got the fake emails. And now the power goes down right after we got the scrubber fixed."

"Mission Control will figure it out," Zoe promised.
"There's nothing we can do from here except keep our
colony safe."

* * *

The entire S.M.A.R.T.S. Mission Control was gathered in the control center. They'd been out of contact with their colonists for almost half an hour. As soon as Jaden, Caleb, Benjamin, and Sonja realized they'd lost communication with the hab, they'd notified Mrs. Ram, Mr. Leavey, and the rest of the team.

The sponsors had immediately gone to find Mr. Pegg. They'd said there was no way they were leaving kids in the hab if there wasn't a way to contact them.

Jaden glanced over at Benjamin. He stood right in front of the flat screen that usually showed the hab's common room. It was as though he thought that if he stared at it hard enough, he could make an image of his twin appear.

"How do you get a baby astronaut to fall asleep?" Jaden asked, hoping a joke would break the tension. Nobody responded. "You rocket," he said, his voice flat.

"Let's go over the facts again. We know the main power source for the hab is solar panels," Caleb said. "It's been sunny all day, so they should be charged, which means the hab should have juice. But somehow the power isn't getting where it should go."

"What if the sunlight didn't get to the panels?" Sonja said. "Mars has tons of dust storms. What if part of the simulation is a simulated dust storm that kept the solar panels from charging?"

"Good thought," Jaden said. "So if the panels are covered with dust, what can we do from here to help?"

"There's the rover." Antonio pointed out. "It has a different power supply. Couldn't we use it to check the panels?"

"I'll try!" yelled Benjamin as he bolted to his console. Everyone gathered around him, watching as he fed in coordinates for the row of solar panels and gave the rover the command to go there.

The kids stared at the screen expectantly.

"We aren't going to know anything for almost half an hour," Jaden reminded them. "It'll take twelve minutes for the rover to get the instructions, and then the video it sends back will be on a twelve-minute delay. At least the rover is close to the panels."

Each minute felt like an hour. It was driving Caleb crazy just standing there. But there was nothing to do but wait.

About twenty minutes later, the door swung open, pulling Caleb's attention away from Benjamin's monitor. Mrs. Ram and Mr. Leavey walked in. Kaylee was with them.

"Good news," Mrs. Ram said. "The power problem is part of the simulation. Everyone in the hab is fine. We had Mr. Pegg show us video."

"Wait, why does *he* have video?" Benjamin protested.

"Because he's watching the simulation, not participating in it," Mr. Leavey explained.

"I don't get why he'd have the power go down," Kaylee said, her rainbow braces flashing as she talked. "Wouldn't that make people think that something is wrong with the habs, that they're not safe?"

"Maybe he wanted to show them how easy it is for colonists — kid colonists — to solve whatever problems come up," Mrs. Ram suggested. "Our team is doing a good job using the backup power for only the most essential hab functions."

"And we just sent the rover to the solar panels to see if there's something wrong with them," Sonja added. "We're waiting for the video."

A few minutes later, an image of the desert and the row of four habs appeared on one of the main screens. The rover rolled slowly toward the solar panels in front of the S.M.A.R.T.S. hab.

"There's something coating the panels," Caleb said, squinting at the screen.

"Hey! There's another rover out there," Sonja pointed out. "Why is someone else's rover coming toward our hab?"

But before anyone could answer, Barrett stormed into the room. "You cheated!" he yelled. "You used your rover to pour sand all over our solar panels so they wouldn't collect any power. We just saw the sand on the video our rover sent back."

Benjamin stood up so fast he knocked his chair over. "That's your rover heading toward our hab right now!" he shouted back. "You're probably having it check whether our panels need more sand or whatever *you* put on them!"

"Please calm down, everyone," Mrs. Ram said firmly. "We're all scientists. Let's not jump to conclusions. Barrett, why do you think our team put sand on your team's panels?"

Barrett shoved a glossy picture at her. "We lost all communication with our hab," he said. "I checked with the Neutrons and the Kelvins. Their power is still fine. So my logical, *scientific* conclusion was that the S.M.A.R.T.S. are sabotaging the Mads to win our competition. I sent our rover out to take pics of our panels. Here's a print. You can see there's sand all over them."

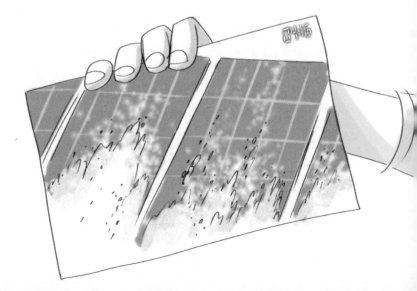

"But there's something on our panels too," Caleb said, gesturing toward the screen.

"Maybe you just did that so you wouldn't look guilty," Barrett argued, but he didn't sound so sure.

"That would hurt our team as much as it'd hurt yours," Jaden pointed out. "It's not like the fake emails. That was something the Mads could have planned together before the colonists went inside the hab. Or something S.M.A.R.T.S. could have planned," he added when Barrett glared at him. "But this is different."

Caleb stepped closer to Jaden. "Benjamin absolutely wouldn't do it, even if he was trying to get Samuel out of the hab," he whispered. "He wouldn't risk being out of contact with his brother."

"Okay . . . so you're innocent this time," Barrett admitted. "Then who did it?"

"Well, it could be part of the simulation," Jaden told him. "Mr. Pegg said the power failure was planned. But it's weird that it only happened to the S.M.A.R.T.S. and the Mads. Why would he put the sand on just our teams' solar panels?"

"Are you sure it's sand on the panels?" Kaylee was looking over Mrs. Ram's shoulder, studying the photo taken by the Mads' rover. "The grains seem too big."

"What does it matter what the stuff is?" Barrett demanded. "It's messing up our teams."

"It might be a clue. Knowing what it is might help us figure out if Mr. Pegg is telling the truth, or if someone else is doing this," Jaden said.

"Then let's get out there," Caleb said.

"We can't," Destiny answered. "Until the simulation ends, that's Mars."

"I'm not part of the simulation. I'll go check it out," Kaylee volunteered. "It could give me a great blog entry!"

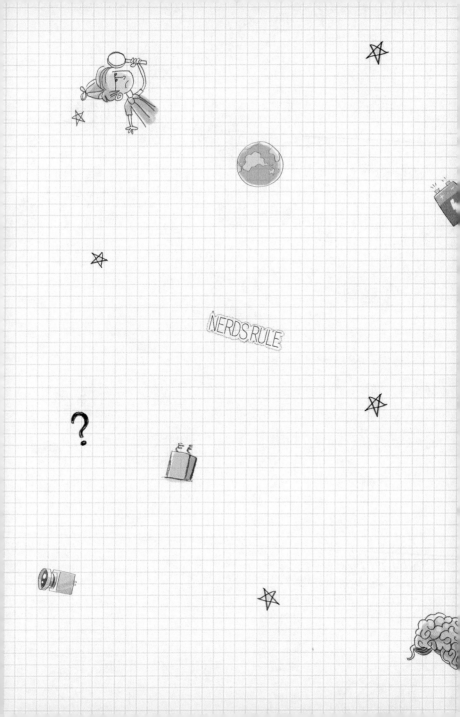

NERDS RULE

?

12

"There's nothing else we can do for the colonists,"
Jaden said thirty minutes later.

Benjamin was using the rover to clean off the solar
panels, but they wouldn't be able to start charging again
until the sun came up. Jaden wasn't even sure the panels
would make enough power to get communication back
before the colonists came out of the hab at lunchtime the
next day.

"We can find out who sabotaged both our teams,"
Barrett said. "We —"

"It isn't sand!" Kaylee announced, interrupting Barrett as she hurried into the S.M.A.R.T.S. control center.

"What is it?" Caleb asked. He and the others crowded around her.

Kaylee set a baggie full of *something* on the back table. "It might be couscous," she said. "I think it's definitely some kind of grain."

Grain! Jaden thought. He had a flash of memory from their conversation with Robin. "Anyone know what quinoa looks like?" he asked.

"I do," Brooke said as she stepped forward and studied the substance. "And that's it!"

"I don't get it. Quinoa on the solar panels — and only on the ones that belong to the S.M.A.R.T.S. and the Mads," said Sonja, crossing her arms. "This can't be part of the simulation. But why would Mr. Pegg lie?"

Caleb thought for a second. "Maybe he doesn't know what's going on, either. He probably lied so that the reporters and investors wouldn't think the Mars colony is dangerous."

"Hold on. What's quinoa?" Barrett demanded.

"Like Kaylee said, it's a kind of grain," Jaden answered. "A locally grown grain." He looked over at Caleb. "You feel like walking around outside? Nothing else we can do here."

"Sure," Caleb replied. Once they were out in the hall, he grinned and added, "If by walking around outside you mean getting proof that the Earth Firsters have been sabotaging us."

They came up to the elevator, and when Jaden pushed the button, the doors opened immediately. Barrett burst in just before they shut again.

"I don't know what's going on," he said. "But it seems like you two know something. I'm not letting you out of my sight until I figure out what."

Jaden tried not to groan. Barrett always yelled first and thought later. He was the anti-Sherlock, but there was no way to get rid of him now.

"We think maybe the Earth Firsters are behind the sabotage," Jaden explained. "They could want to make the Mars Commission look bad in front of the reporters and possible investors."

"One of them, this girl Robin, had a thing of Cheez Crunchies in her bag," Caleb added as the elevator doors opened on the ground floor. "And we found out they eat a lot of quinoa. But we don't have any proof they did anything yet."

"Unacceptable! *I'll* get a confession," Barrett promised. He led the way outside. "Just show me which one she is."

The Earth Firsters were back to marching around with their signs and yelling their slogans. Jaden spotted Robin right away, but he wasn't sure he wanted to tell Barrett that.

"Hey! Hey, you guys!" a girl called.

Robin's sister, Lark, was running toward them. "Can I borrow a cell phone? Just for a few minutes. Pleasepleaseplease. Please!" She looked over her shoulder, then ducked behind the boys. Caleb was sure she was trying to hide from her sister.

"I'll let you use mine if you answer a couple questions for us," Jaden said.

Lark held out her hand. Jaden put his cell in her palm.

"Is that Robin?" Barrett demanded.

Jaden was silent for a moment, staring at Lark as she pulled up the game on his phone. "No. Forget about finding Robin," he told Barrett. "I just realized she didn't do it — nobody from Earth First did."

"How do you figure?" Caleb asked.

Jaden glanced at Lark. "Can't you play your game on a laptop?" he asked.

"As if I'd be let near one of those," Lark said, not taking her eyes off the little screen. "No one in Earth First has a computer."

A light bulb turned on in Caleb's brain. "No cells phones, no computers, no way to

send the fake emails. The Earth Firsters can't be behind the sabotage."

"And we already agreed neither of our teams did it," Barrett said, crossing his arms. "So who's the perp?"

* * *

When Jaden, Caleb, and Barrett returned to S.M.A.R.T.S. Mission Control, it was empty.

"They must have gone up to the suite," Jaden said. "Without a way to communicate with the colonists, there's nothing to do in here."

The three boys took the elevator up to the top floor. As they expected, they found the rest of the S.M.A.R.T.S. kids there — and everyone from the Mad Scientists' control center!

"We're reading some of Kaylee's blog, since there's nothing we can do for the colonists right now," Sonja told them, like it was normal to be hanging out with the rival team.

"Kaylee didn't come up with you?" Caleb asked, looking around.

"She said she was going to tell the other reporters about the quinoa," Amanda, one of the Mads who'd been extra friendly on the bus, answered. "I think she wanted to gloat. She got the story before all the adults."

"Her blog is really popular," Sonja commented. "She got more than four-hundred thousand hits today! People are really into the Mars Commission project. Some think it's awesome. Some think it'll be a disaster. But they all want more info on the simulation, and Kaylee's been blasting new content onto her site."

"Well, she has been filming constantly," Antonio reminded them.

"She also gets stuff up fast. She had the quinoa post up an hour ago. And just before that, she posted about how Mr. Pegg lied when he said the power outage was part of the simulation. Really he had no idea what happened," Sonja continued.

"She had a post up about our competition almost as soon as we got here," Caroline, the Mads girl who loved bad jokes as much as Jaden, added. "And she wrote about the sabotage and how the Mads and the S.M.A.R.T.S. were blaming each other. Tons of people commented on those."

"Wait. You said she had the quinoa post up an hour ago?" Jaden asked. His Spidey senses were really tingling now.

"Yeah," Sonja said. She checked the blog. "At 4:02 p.m."

"Does anyone remember what time we sent the rover out to check the panels?" Jaden asked.

Barrett pulled the picture taken by the Mads' rover out of his pocket and checked the time stamp. "Our rover checked our panels at 4:16."

"So Kaylee put up a post about the quinoa more than fourteen minutes before she supposedly went out to check the solar panels," Jaden said.

Caleb could practically feel the neurons in his brain light up. "So unless she can time travel, that means she's the one who put the quinoa on the panels! This whole time she's been creating stories to put on her blog so she'd get more readers!"

"A new post just went up," Sonja announced. "It's about how the Earth Firsters are sabotaging the simulation."

"That makes the story even better," Jaden commented. "And it makes Kaylee look really smart. She solved the mystery."

"I can't believe it," Finn, another of the Mads' kids, said. "She actually got us to believe we were sabotaging each other."

"She was with us when Mr. Pegg brought us into the building. She saw how much Samuel hated the sound of cracking knuckles and how Barrett did it to bug him,"

Jaden pointed out. "So when she emailed from the fake account, she told Zoe to crack her knuckles."

"Let's go get her!" Barrett exclaimed.

"Let's go get *proof*," Jaden said. "And I have an idea on how to do it. We need to find Lark."

"That should be easy," Caleb said. "Just go outside and wave a cell phone around."

* * *

"Got it!" Lark called. She trotted toward the bench outside the Mars Commission building where Caleb, Jaden, and Barrett were waiting for her.

Finding Lark had been just as easy as Caleb had predicted. Jaden had offered her a deal — if she could convince Kaylee to loan Lark her cell phone for five minutes, Jaden would let the girl use his phone until they went home. He was sure she'd be able to do it. He'd seen her begging in action.

"Trade you!" Lark said, eyes sparkling.

Jaden gave her his phone, and he took Kaylee's. "We'll give it back," he said, but Lark had wandered off, already playing her game. Jaden hit the email icon on Kaylee's phone. "Good. She's still logged on."

"You're going to read her email?" Caleb asked.

Jaden hesitated. "I just want to see if she set up that fake Mars Commission email account. I'm not going to read any personal stuff."

"I'll do it!" Barrett said, snatching the phone. A few seconds later, he grinned. "Oh, yeah. Here's a receipt for the domain name marscommisssion.com — with the extra *s*."

"And once she had the domain name, she could set up email accounts with the fake address," Caleb said.

Barrett rubbed his hands together. "I can't wait to tell that blogger that we caught her. I'll be like, 'In your face, Kaylee!' Let's go!"

"Actually, there are a few other people we should tell first," Jaden said, smiling. "I think it's time for the other reporters covering the simulation to get a scoop of their own."

NERDS RULE

?

13

On Monday afternoon, Zoe, Goo, Samuel, and Dylan stood in front of the airlock. It was finally time to leave the hab. They hadn't been able to complete all their experiments since they'd had to save power, but they'd kept the essential hab systems running. They had survived Mars.

The door swung open smoothly. Mr. Pegg stood by the entrance, one of his frighteningly wide smiles on his face. There was also a crowd of people waiting — reporters, potential investors, and the Mission Control groups for all four teams.

Underneath their cheers, Zoe thought she could hear people chanting "Earth First! Earth First!" But their voices couldn't compete.

Zoe spotted Jaden and Caleb and raced over to them. She had a million questions to ask them and a million things to tell them about living like a colonist. But before she could say anything, Jaden handed her a stack of newspapers from that morning, a big grin on his face.

Zoe scanned the headlines: "Blogger Falsifies Story," "Simulation Sabotage," "Sabotage for a Scoop" — they were all accompanied by pictures of Kaylee.

Zoe stared at one of the pictures. In it, the blogger was trying to shield her face from the camera with one hand. She looked like she wanted to disappear.

"Kaylee sent the fake emails?" Zoe asked, skimming the first few paragraphs of one of the articles.

"Yeah. She also snuck the Crunchies in Samuel's bag while you were touring the hab," Caleb said.

"I saw her get an orange streak on her shirt when she used it to wipe off her phone! That must have been Crunchies gunk!" Zoe said. "But why'd she want us to think the Mads were sabotaging us?"

"All she cared about was getting great stories for her blog. So she did everything she could to create drama," Jaden explained.

"That's why she wanted the Mads to think we were sabotaging them too," Caleb added. "Then when she'd played that story out, she tried to make it look like the Earth Firsters had sabotaged both teams by putting quinoa on the solar panels."

"We thought there was something wrong with the panels," Zoe exclaimed. "Samuel was great. As soon as we switched to emergency backup power, he had us shut down everything that wasn't essential."

"Really? Benjamin was a nutball," Caleb told her. "For a while we thought he was behind the sabotage because he wanted Samuel out of the hab."

Zoe laughed. "Maybe it was good for them to spend some time apart."

"Still, they look pretty happy to be back together." Jaden nodded at Benjamin and Samuel. The twins were in front of the hab, taking selfies with their arms around each other's shoulders.

"In the hab, did you —" Caleb began.

Zoe held up her hand to stop him. "First, I've got to know if the sponsors have decided who won the contest."

"They didn't decide. But we did," Caleb answered.

Zoe frowned. "We who?"

"The S.M.A.R.T.S. and Mad Scientists Mission Control teams," he said. "We hung out together while we were waiting for the simulation to end. There wasn't a lot for us to do, since we couldn't communicate with the habs."

"So . . . who won?" Zoe asked.

"It's a tie," Jaden told her. "Both teams were sabotaged, and both teams did a good job dealing with it. Plus we solved the mystery together."

"Sounds good to me!" Zoe replied. She raised her eyebrows. "Barrett must be mad, though. He really, really wanted to beat us."

"You're not going to believe this," Jaden said. "But calling the contest a tie was Barrett's idea."

"So, are we like *friends* with him now?" Zoe looked over at Barrett, who was standing with the Mads and Mr. Olsen.

Caleb nudged Jaden, smiling. "Did you hear that? I think Zoe had a breakdown in there. She just asked if we're friends with Barrett."

"After Barrett said he thought the contest should be a tie, he told us we'll have to make them the biggest trophy ever," Jaden told her. "Then he promised the Mads would destroy us if we ever dared go up against them again."

Zoe laughed. "I'm glad planet Earth didn't change too much while I was gone."

About the Author

Melinda Metz is the author of more than sixty
books for teens and kids, including *Echoes* and the
young adult series Roswell High, the basis of the
TV show *Roswell*. Her middle-grade mystery *Wright
and Wong: Case of the Nana-Napper* (co-authored by
the fabulous Laura J. Burns) was a juvenile Edgar
finalist. Melinda lives in Concord, North Carolina,
with her dog, Scully, a pen-eater just like the dog who
came before her.

About the Illustrator

Heath McKenzie is a best-selling author and illustrator
from Melbourne, Australia. Over the course of his
career, he has illustrated numerous books, magazines,
newspapers, and even live television. As a child, Heath
was often inventing things, although his inventions
didn't always work out as planned. His inventions still
only work some of the time . . . but that's the fun of
experimenting!

Glossary

colony (KAH-luh-nee) — a group of people sent to live in and settle a new territory

essential (i-SEN-shuhl) — very important and necessary

habitat (HAB-uh-tat) — a structure that provides shelter, air, controlled temperature, and other necessities so that humans can live in places that would otherwise be impossible to survive; also called a hab

module (MOJ-ool) — a self-contained unit that can work by itself but is also a part of a larger spacecraft

perp (PURP) — short for perpetrator; a perpetrator is someone who has committed a crime

quinoa (KEEN-wah) — seeds from a tall crop plant used as food or ground into flour

rover (ROH-ver) — a vehicle designed to travel across planets or moons

sabotage (SAB-uh-tahzh) — to deliberately damage or destroy something so that it no longer works correctly

scrubber (SKRUHB-er) — a device that removes harmful substances from air or water

simulation (sim-yuh-LAY-shuhn) — something that looks, feels, and behaves like a specific situation or process; a simulation is often used for study or to train people

suspect (SUHS-pekt) — a person who might have done something wrong and is being investigated

Discussion Questions

1. The Earth First group was protesting against the Mars Commission. Why do they think people shouldn't spend money on a Mars colony? Look back at the text, then explain why using your own words. Do you agree with the Earth Firsters?

2. Would you rather be a Mars colonist or a member of Mission Control? Talk about the reasons behind your choice.

3. Jaden and Caleb had a lot of suspects to investigate. When you were reading, who did you think was the perp? Discuss what made each person a suspect, including the facts that made them look guilty and the reasons why they might have wanted to sabotage the teams.

Writing Prompts

1. Benjamin and Samuel usually do everything together, but they split up for the Mars mission. Write two paragraphs that compare and contrast how the twins felt during the simulation. How did Benjamin feel? How did Samuel feel? Use examples from the story to support your answer.

2. Write your own blog post! Tell readers how Kaylee sabotaged the S.M.A.R.T.S. and the Mad Scientists. Don't forget to explain why she did it!

3. Although Zoe was excited to be a colonist, living in the hab wasn't always easy. Make a list of things that would be hard about living on Mars, and then write a list about what would be good or exciting. Looking at your lists, would you become a Mars colonist? Why or why not? Write a paragraph about your decision.

Space Colonization

Space colonization, also called space settlement, is the process of creating permanent places off of Earth for humans to live. Colonies could be set up on places like moons, planets, or asteroids. A colony could also live in a man-made structure, such as an orbiting space station.

There are a lot of problems to solve before living in space becomes a reality. One of the biggest challenges is cost. It's expensive to develop and build the technology, train colonists, gather supplies, and rocket everything millions of miles into space. A single trip would costs billions of dollars. And once colonists arrive, they would have to deal with a deadly environment. Other planets don't have an atmosphere that provides breathable air and protection against radiation, moderate temperatures, food, or water the way Earth does.

Despite the challenges, different groups continue to work toward space colonization. Government agencies such as the National Aeronautics and Space Administration (NASA) and the European Space Agency (ESA) develop advanced space technology. And companies such as SpaceX and Virgin Galactic want to make spaceflight safer and cheaper so people can take vacations in space. An organization called Mars One even wants to put a colony on Mars by 2027.

Some scientists, including famed cosmologist Stephen Hawking, think space colonization is essential for our survival. They fear we will one day destroy our planet through war or by using up all its natural resources. Others interested in space colonies can't resist the adventure of living among the stars. In any case, we should do our best to care for Earth because it'll be difficult to find anywhere that's as good as our home planet.

More adventure and science mysteries!

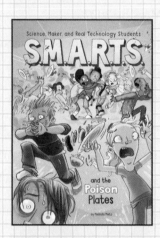
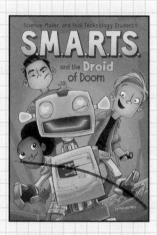

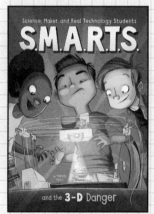